BUBBA
AND
BABBA

BUBBA AND BABBA

Based on a Russian Folktale
MARIA POLUSHKIN

Pictures by
Diane de Groat

CROWN PUBLISHERS, INC., NEW YORK

Manufactured in the United States of America
Published simultaneously in Canada by General Publishing
Company Limited. 10 9 8 7 6 5 4 3 2

The text of this book is set in 16 point Souvenir Medium.
The illustrations are charcoal drawings, printed in three
colors, with overlays prepared by the artist.

Library of Congress Cataloging in Publication Data

Polushkin, Maria.
   Bubba and Babba: story.

   SUMMARY: Two lazy bears go to great lengths to avoid
work, especially around the house.
   [1. Laziness—Fiction]   I. de Groat, Diane.
II. Title.
PZ7.P7695Bu   [E]   75-15914
ISBN 0-517-52435-X

gratefully, to Norma Jean

This is the story of two very lazy bears. One bear was named Bubba and the other was called Babba. They were so lazy that they argued all day long about who was to do what.

When they got up in the morning, Bubba said to Babba, "You must make the beds this morning, for I made them yesterday." Babba said, "What is the point of making the beds, when in the evening we must unmake them? But Bubba, today you must sweep the floor, because I did it yesterday." "Why should I sweep the floor when it will only get dirty again? Why don't we just leave it as it is?"

They didn't make the beds and they didn't
sweep the floor, but went out for a walk in the
warm sunshine. As they were walking, they
came to a field of lovely flowers. "Oh, these
flowers are so beautiful," said Babba, "I wish
you would pick some so we could have them in
the house."

"I don't mind flowers," said Bubba, "but if I
pick them and take them home, they will only
wilt, so why bother?"

They walked along a little farther and
came across a farmer mowing hay.

"Hello, farmer," they said.

"Hello, bears," he replied.

"You have come just in time. If you will help me with the mowing, I will repay you with a dozen eggs from my best chickens."

The bears thought about this for a moment and then Bubba said, "Thank you very much, but we should have to work very hard for those eggs, and then we should have to carry them all the way home, and perhaps on the way they would break, so it would all be for nothing. No, I think we shall lie down under this tree and take a little rest. Nothing is quite so pleasant as watching someone else toil while doing nothing yourself."

When the bears got home from their walk, Bubba said, "I am getting quite hungry from all that exercise." "Yes, I am too," said Babba. "Now the sun is setting and it is getting cold. I am afraid that one of us will have to make supper and one of us will have to chop wood for a fire."

As they could think of no way to get around doing these chores, Bubba went to chop some wood and Babba cooked some porridge for their supper.

After they had eaten the porridge, Bubba sat back, wiped his mouth and said, "That was quite delicious, Babba. Now I will sit in front of our lovely fire while you clean up the dishes."

"You will do nothing of the kind, Bubba.
I made this porridge and by all rights you must
clean up the dishes."

"My dear Babba, you are all wrong. For while you were cooking, I chopped all this wood and that was a much harder job. So you must do the cleaning up."

"Bubba, you are being quite unfair and most unpleasant. *Everyone* knows that the one who cooks should not have to do the dishes. So please stop arguing and do them."

"I will not. You will," said Bubba.
"And I most certainly will not. You will,"
  shouted Babba.

"I will not either.

YOU WILL!"
screamed Bubba.

"NO! YOU WILL!"

They shouted at each other for a long time, but neither one would give in. After a while they sat down and just looked at each other. Finally Babba said,

"I HAVE AN IDEA!

Let's leave the dishes tonight and go to bed. Whoever gets up first in the morning and is the first to speak will wash the dishes." Bubba thought that was a great idea, and they went happily off to bed.

When the sun came up the next morning, it was a beautiful warm day. The birds were singing and the squirrels were running up and down trees, chattering. But inside the bears' house no one stirred. Bubba and Babba lay in their beds and pretended to be asleep, for neither one wanted to be the first to get up.

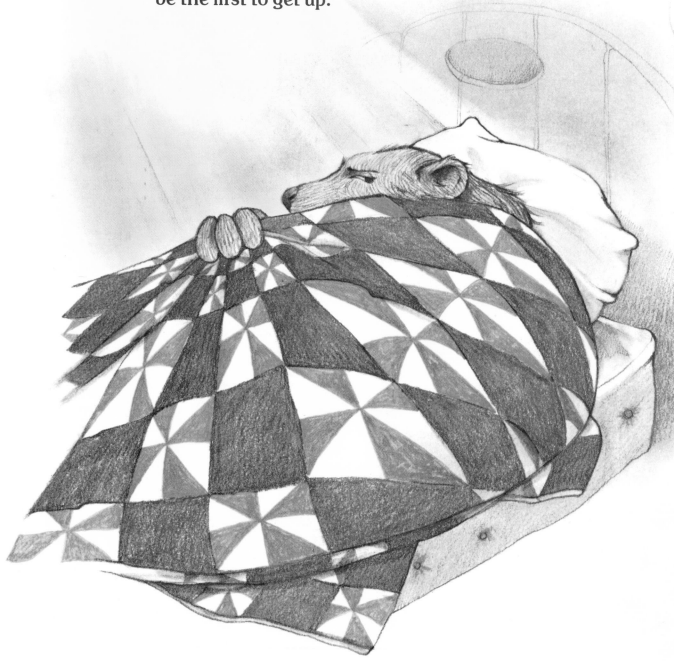

"This is just fine
with me,"
thought Bubba.

"Nothing like a long stay in bed." "I hate getting
up in the morning, so I will just turn over and go
back to sleep," thought Babba.

The morning went by and now the sun was
high overhead. Every once in a while, Bubba
would peek through his tightly shut eyes to see if
Babba was stirring, but Babba was lying just as
quietly as Bubba.

The afternoon went by, and though it was now quite late, the two lazy bears were still in bed pretending to be asleep. Suddenly there was a knock on the door. It was Raccoon, come to pay them a visit. When he knocked again and there was no answer, he decided to come in and leave them a note. He walked into the kitchen and saw last night's dirty dishes lying on the table. "Ugh. What a mess," he said. "I think I will surprise them and clean it all up. Perhaps by the time I'm done, they will return."

Both Bubba and Babba heard someone puttering around in the kitchen. By this time they were not even pretending to be asleep anymore, but were lying with their eyes bugging out of their heads, trying so hard not to speak.

They heard the clatter of the dishes, and they
heard someone humming, and they heard the
whistling of the teakettle, and finally, when they
could not be quiet one second more, both bears
jumped out of bed and shouted,

"Who is it?"

"Who is in
our kitchen?"

Raccoon was so startled that he dropped
the bowls he had been putting back on the
shelf. When Bubba and Babba saw their
friend and the broken bowls, they both
sat down and laughed for a long time.
Finally Babba said, "We are two silly
bears. I am starving and I have never
been so bored in all my life." And
Bubba said, "I have a headache and
have never had so many bad dreams
in all my life. Let us both try not to be
so lazy anymore."

Then they all sat down and had
some breakfast, which was silly
because it was already dinnertime.